Francis Fontaine

Etowah

A Romance of the Confederacy

Francis Fontaine

Etowah
A Romance of the Confederacy

ISBN/EAN: 9783337346874

Printed in Europe, USA, Canada, Australia, Japan

Cover: Foto ©Andreas Hilbeck / pixelio.de

More available books at **www.hansebooks.com**

ETOWAH.

A Romance of the Confederacy.

DEDICATION.

To the disabled Confederate veterans, this book is respectfully dedicated by a fellow-soldier, with the hope that it may be the means of inaugurating a practical sympathy for them commensurate with their necessities.

You confronted nearly three millions of enlisted men, during four years of the bloodiest war on record, with a patriotism and heroism unsurpassed in history. Of these 3,000,000 men, enlisted in the armies of the United States, 303,843 were killed during the war, and the average of killed and wounded in battle, on one side or the other, frequently exceeded thirty per cent. of the forces engaged.

Neither Waterloo nor Wagram, nor Lodi, nor any of the great battles fought by Napoleon, show as great percentage of losses as the battles of the Wilderness and Spottsylvania, Chicamauga and Atlanta, Gettysburg or Shiloh.

At Gettysburg, Pennsylvania, 54,000 men fell; at Chicamauga, Georgia, 33,000 men were killed and wounded. Malice can find no lasting place in a hero's heart, and these figures are presented, not to revive bitter memories of the past, but that the reader may appreciate the enormous number of helpless, aged, and cripple veterans throughout the Southern States. While twelve millions of dollars a month are paid as pensions to the Federal soldiers, whether wounded or not, no government pensions these Southern soldiers, and no public charities have been organized for their benefit.

LET VETERAN'S HOMES BE BUILT FOR THOSE THAT ARE HELPLESS.

Philanthropy had never a nobler field of labor, and a patriot's gratitude cannot find more worthy recipients than these maimed heroes who yielded all in defence of their country.

We of the South, owe it to them as a sacred duty, and the

great heart of the American people will esteem it a debt worthily bestowed.

> " The soldier's spirit greets the soldier's call,
> There is no hate between the brave and brave,
> And he whose hand in battle labored first,
> When darkness falls will labor first to save."

As a slight contribution to building a Veteran's Home in the city of Atlanta, Georgia, one-half of the proceeds of this book will be applied to that purpose.

PREFACE.

SCENE.—*A Book-store in New York City.*

VISITOR—"Have you any book treating of the negro as a slave and as a freedman and citizen? Any book that describes the domestic life of the Southern people under the *régime* of slavery?"

BOOKSELLER—"Oh, yes, 'Uncle Tom's Cabin' is very popular."

VISITOR—"I know that, and deservedly so. I have seen that book all over Europe, translated into half a dozen languages. But that treats of slavery as it was thought to be by the Abolitionists before the late war between the States; it describes the horrors, but not the brighter phases of slavery."

BOOKSELLER—"We have 'The Impending Crisis,' by Helper. It was recommended for circulation by sixty-eight members of Congress, and also by the Secretary of State, when it was published."

VISITOR—"That is not what I want, either. Like 'Uncle Tom's Cabin,' it pandered to the prejudices of the Abolitionists and advocated the confiscation of slave property without compensation to the owners. It used the following language, which shows the animus of the book:

'Frown, sirs; fret, foam, prepare your weapons, threaten, strike, shoot, stab, bring on civil war; dissolve the Union. You can neither foil nor intimidate us; we have determined to abolish slavery, and, so help us God, abolish it we will! Compensation to slave-owners for negroes! Preposterous idea; the suggestion is criminal, the demand unjust, wicked, damnable, monstrous. Shall we fee the curs of slavery to make them rich at our expense?'

Such is the language used. That is not what I want."

BOOKSELLER—"Then what do you want? Ah! I have it, 'The Fool's Errand' will suit you."

VISITOR—"No; I have read that, too. That is worse than the others, because it is written by a 'carpet-bagger' who settled in the South after the war to make all he could for himself out of the woes of an impoverished and disheartened people. What I want to find is a book which will show the South as it was and is - the domestic life and customs of the people, both white and black, both slave and free—a book written to give the true history of that remarkable struggle, which so puzzled foreigners, without pandering to Northern or Southern prejudices."

BOOKSELLER—"There is no such book printed, and, in my judgment, there will never be. You may as well give up the search."

VISITOR (*sotto voce*)—"We will see. Such a book is needed, and I will write it."

And thus this unpretentious book has been written that the reader may appreciate the motives which actuated the Southern States in seceding from the Union.

In the light of experience, sufficient time has already passed to justify the assertion that the great Republic has been purified in the fiery crucible of war.

It is also evident that the Southern States, in the next half century, will have advaned far more in all the arts, sciences, and appliances of civilization without slavery than with it. But one can read all the histories from Northern sources that have been written, and in none of them will be found the unprejudiced, truthful description of the motives, sacrifices, triumphs and losses of the Southern people during the four years of war between the States. To give a faithful picture of life as it was under the *régime* of slavery, "with malice to none and charity for all," the author submits this simple story to the public.

Later Colonel Leslie and his son, Hugh, arrived just as he cannon sounded the signal for illuminating the city.

In an instant the houses gleamed with lights, the streets and squares became brilliant with bonfires and fire-works, which recalled to the returned tourists the famous *Champs Elysées* in Paris.

Pedestrians thronged the street, and young men flung their Zouave caps, or hats adorned with cockades, high in the air.

Had it been in Paris, this day of hilarious revolution would have been ushered in with bloodshed, and hired *claqueurs* would have mounted the walls, and statues, and trees, and led the populace in wild cries of *"Vive l' Empereur!"*

But in this distant Southern State there was no monarch to welcome to power, no ruler to overthrow, and no personal animosities to gratify.

It seemed absolutely unanimous; the old and the young, the rich and the poor, the high and the humble, the slave and the free, all joined in the carnival of enthusiasm.

The little group had ascended to the top of the mansion, one of the largest and finest in the city, and had a fine view of the whole town.

"Oh, how beautiful it is!" said Clara Leslie, full of the enthusiasm of a girl of sixteen years. "Indeed, it is prettier than the illumination during the *fêtes in Paris.*"

"Is it really?" said Julia. "Oh! how I do long to visit foreign lands."

"Why, Miss Julia," said Latané, you boasted this afternoon that you *had* visited a foreign land."

"And so we did when we crossed the river; but that is not like Europe, and, above all, it is not like Paris."

"C'est bien vrai, ne c'est pas, ma bien aimée?" said Hugh Leslie, as he looked down into the eyes of Nathalie Blanc, a lovely daughter of one of the oldest Creole families in New Orleans.

"Oui, Monsieur, décidément," she answered.

"What are you two talking about?" said Julia Dearing, who had just heard enough to know that they were speaking French.

"I said that Paris was the pupil of the eye of the world," said Hugh, not wishing to reveal what he had said.

"And I that it was second only to New Orleans. I am always loyal to my home," responded Miss Blanc.

"That reminds me what it is that makes this scene so brilliant and so attractive to me: it is because it beautifies our own homes. How glad I shall be to see my old home again," said Clara.

"Home, home! sweet, sweet home!

"The dearest spot on earth to me is home," said Henry Latané, humming the air.

"Oh! do let us sing it!" said Julia, and in a moment those clear young voices sang the familiar air with a zest that was so charming that Colonel Leslie and Judge Dearing paused to listen until it was finished before ascending the last flight of stairs to the top of the house. This house, by the way, was a typical Southern home. The front was ornamented by lofty Ionic columns that reached to the roof, and a broad piazza ran the length of the mansion. It contained fourteen large rooms with wide halls on every floor, but the promenade on top of the house was the most unique and, in summer, the most delightful feature. It was finished throughout in hard woods, and the whole lower floor could be converted into a ball-room by throwing back the massive mahogany sliding-doors.

Hardly had they ceased singing when a band of students appeared in the square below, and halted on the lawn which led from the residence of Judge Dearing to the river.

Then Clara Leslie and Nathalie Blanc heard for the first time the stirring strains of the Southern *Marséillaise*, and ere they knew it they had caught the refrain and were joining in the chorus:

"In Dixie's land I'll take my stand
And live and die in Dixie."

And so did the little urchins in the streets, and so did the crowd which made a motley assemblage, until the whole square resounded with the martial air, and the enthusiasm became unbounded.

Colonel Leslie turned and grasped the hand of the venerable Judge, and said:

"I feel as if I, too, could throw my hat in the air."

Henry Latané, noticing this, said:

"Hugh, do you intend to enter the Military Institute again?"

"I don't know. Father and I were talking of it as we drove into town this evening. 1 think I will go into the army immediately. By the way, what has become of Barnum?"

"He is captain of company 'C,' of the Cadet Corps. Do you remember him?"

"Very well, and very favorably—a better fellow I never knew. But, if my memory is not at fault, he is from the State of New York?"

"You are correct, and I agree with you in your good opinion of him."

"How does he take this sort of thing?" said Hugh, waving his hand toward the enthusiastic groups in the square and in the streets below them.

The stand at the race-course was thronged with lovely women and manly men. The afternoon was delightful, the warm atmosphere being tempered by the soft spring breezes that caressed the cheeks of maidens, whose color rivalled that of the rose. The bright blue skies were relieved by alpine-like cumulus clouds which, if they did not seem to have motion, would be perfect re-productions of the snow-clad peaks amid the Alps. The last race is finished, and at her waist hangs the trophy won by Nathalie Blanc from Hugh Leslie. A handkerchief, on which was embroidered an ideal flag of the new nation, designed and executed by Julia Dearing, with only three stars as yet, though space was left for a dozen more, was in the happy possession of Bruton Stewart as an evidence of his success in betting on Latané's blooded mare against his own thoroughbred which Julia had championed. And a close observer might have seen the shy, sweet glance that Clara Leslie gave to Latané, as he received from Julia's hand the little curl which she clipped from the wealth of hair—golden and luxuriant tresses that well could spare it—and which indicated that he had won the rarest prize of all. At least Latané so considered it, for he said:

"I shall have a locket made which shall be the shrine for this—"

"Love-lock," interrupted Julia, with a mischievous smile.

"No, 'love-lock' is purely a masculine appendage," said Stewart. "It was worn by men of fashion in the reign of Queen Elizabeth—worn on the forehead, not on the heart. Look you! Latané, let us guard our rights as men, and rigidly taboo the wearing of 'love-locks' by the fair, sweet sex."

The bugles sounded for the "knights" to assemble for the Tourney as this speech was made, and Hugh Leslie, Latané and Stewart, with a dozen other young gentlemen from various parts of the grand stand, bade a hasty adieu to their young lady friends, and descended to enter the lists.

A dozen young ladies might have been seen then to pin a ribbon, each of a different color, and each contrasting well with the dress selected for this occasion, so that, when she arose, her "knight" might see the emblem which was to cheer him to victory. And now, below them, "pools" are being sold for the final race which is to succeed the tournament; for all the *élite* of the county is there, and no county in America, perhaps, thus distant from a large city, could boast of horses more famed for pedigree and swiftness than that of Etowah.

Each "knight" was required by the club rules to ride his own horse, and that the horse should be of a well-known pedigree. It was thus that they kept out of the lists, without giving offense, men who might be accomplished riders but were not of their "set." Thus in the middle ages the title of "knight" or "cavalier" was limited to persons of noble birth. A light mask was worn by each knight, and an imitation of the armor worn by the knights of old was usually worn so as to complete the disguise and render the spectacle more attractive. By their colors they were known by the wearers of the ribbons. The silver tones of a cornet announced their egress from the round-house, or place of assemblage, and the prancing steeds seemed eager for a race around the course rather than a tilt at the rings. It was indeed a pleasing spectacle as they rode forth and passed the grand stand, each "knight" doffing his plumed hat as he passed the lady who wore his colors.

Stewart was recognized by his great stature and herculean strength, and the applause of the multitude greeted him as he rode forth. But his eyes were cast to where Julia Dearing sat, and he waved the handkerchief toward her as he saw her pin the ribbon to her dress.

"By George! Stewart," said Latané, "I believe you have won the fight already!"

"Not so, Latané; I received my 'walking papers' this morning, but I am going to win this contest, crown her as queen of beauty, and shake the dust of this State from my feet." There was no time for further conversation; the bugles sounded the charge, and away, one after another, the knights, each with lance well poised, dashed for the twenty consecutive rings.

Eighteen rings were on the lance held proudly aloft by

Stewart, as he approached the beginning point, and cries of "Hurrah for the Halbardier!" resounded.

He was dressed like an ancient Halbardier, and his lance was very like the halbard, an ancient military weapon, consisting of a pole or shaft of wood, having a head armed with a steel point, with a cross-piece of steel.

He had won the choice of position and being in the lead, had taken all the rings but two, which were taken by the third man on the list, a "knight" who bore the name "Unknown." Had not betting on the results of the tournament been prohibited by the rules of the club, a large amount would have been placed on the success of Stewart, now the general favorite, and well did Julia assume the rôle alloted to her, though in her heart she regretted that she would probably have to be publicly congratulated on being crowned as "queen of love and beauty" by the gentleman whom she had rejected as a suitor that day.

"Etowah Heights," his ancestral home, was the finest estate in the county, and Stewart was, in all respects, worthy her favorable consideration.

Her vanity was flattered by his persistent decision to appear to be her devoted admirer until he left with his troop for "the front," as the seat of probable war was already styled in Virginia.

The fourth knight chose as his device "The Talisman;" and none felt its significance more deeply than the young girl whose tiny lock of hair had in two hours caused him to change his costume and title that he might adapt himself to the incident.

"Count Robert, of Paris," "Ivanhoe," and other famous knights of the middle ages, were the prototypes selected by the various competitors. The knight who bore on his crest the word "Unknown" was Hugh Leslie, who was thought to be still abroad. except by a few intimate friends, for in those days the arrival or departure of prominent people was not chronicled in the daily gazette; their names paraded side by side with that of the family baker or milliner anxious to chronicle their departure for "the springs." Nor were the minute descriptions of the dresses of the belles at parties considered proper subjects for newspaper criticism. They were trained in a different social school, and were averse to "staleing their presence before the vulgar herd." The members of the club which supported the race-course and tournament festivals retained for their families the privilege accorded to the ancient cavaliers, that of occupying during the races or public sports the first fourteen tiers or rows of seats. The cavaliers of the middle ages alone possessed the right to carry a banner, and to appear in the tourneys and contest for the prize; to wear gilded armor and a collar of gold; to place a vane upon their manor houses; to have a particular seal upon their coat-of-arms; to take the title of *monseigneur*, and their wives of *madame*. In exchange for these prerogatives, they swore to combat injustice everywhere, to be the defenders of the orphan and the widow, and to obey without reserve the orders of their lady or of their king. Thus the glorious history of this institution during the crusades in the Holy Land; thus the most ameliorating conditions of feudal times; thus the order of the Good Templars, the Legion of Honor, the Hospitaliers, and the "Sir Knights," which distingush the members of the brotherhood of to-day which have the same objects in view. Originated at a time when the strong hand was the only law, brave men took upon themselves the task of protecting the weak and redressing the wrongs of the injured. Women, being the weakest and most apt to suffer wrong, were first protected, and thus courtesy and refinement were blended with courage, and to be a knight was to be the champion of the oppressed. But chivalry had nothing to do with any but those of gentle birth, and the dogma that "all men are, and of right ought to be, created free and equal," had not been proclaimed. A knight would protect his vassals as he would his horse, but he did not appreciate that the common people had any rights if opposed to his will.

War was his profession; trade he could not indulge in without forfeiture of his social position and his feudal rights. The chase, tournaments, and other sports, which developed manly strength and courteous courage, were his amusements. Tournaments were held under the auspices of the King or a great noble, and were attended by ladies who bestowed the prizes won by the successful combatants. Again the bugles sound and away the contestants go, the 'Halbardier' now in the rear, and Hugh Leslie in front, and as they approach the stand it is seen that seventeen rings grace his lance, and the 'Unknown' is cheered vociferously. Nathalie Blanc has arisen from her seat and claps her hands as she sees her knight take ring after ring, but her pleasure is moderated when she learns that he lacks one ring of being equal to Stewart. "Oh! Julia, I fear you have won!" she said.

Again the bugles sound, and with a grace that is marked by all, Latané leads. A shout that makes the stand tremble arises, as the graceful youth holds his lance aloft and it is seen that he has taken every ring!

One after one, they all essay again until the time for the final effort of the young giant, Stewart, arrives. For the second time he advances, and after him comes no other. Thirty-eight rings stand to the credit of Latané, for only two were taken by his predecessors in the last run, and he secured all the rest.

The tilt is between Latané and Stewart. In his excitement Stewart has let fall his mask, and few are as popular as he in the county. People rise on their feet, heads are bent forward and eyes are strained to see the champion make his final thrust. In unison with the crowd around them, our young friends also arose, and when it is seen that the most fearless equestrienne and the handsomest girl in the county, Miss Julia Dearing, wears his colors, the excitement increases and murmurs of admiration are heard.

"What a handsome couple they will make!" is the remark.

Bruton Stewart, a proud smile upon his lips, rides forward, stops for a moment just below the group in which Miss Dearing is the central figure, lifts his hat and bows with that grace for which West Point graduates have become famous. With irresistible impulse Julia Dearing unpins the ribbon and waves it to him.

In a moment he is off, and voices cry "one!" "two!!" "three!!!" and so on, until the fifteenth ring is reached, as the people count as he secures each ring Surely he will win! The sympathy of the spectators is with the superb young cavalry leader, who returned but a month ago from West Point, and already has organized a cavalry regiment and will leave next week for Virginia.

"Hurrah! Hurrah!" resounds on every side, as fast as he takes the rings.

Julia Dearing is excited as she never was before. Exulting in his success she could not help admiring the superb, reckless, daring and graceful carriage of her champion, and she began to wonder if she had not made a mistake in rejecting so gallant a cavalier. But could she have seen the proud, scornful look upon his face, she would have realized that no effort could ever again make Bruton Stewart a suppliant for her favor.

It was the look of a man who scorned the very success he was achieving in securing these harmless rings; it was the look of a man who courts death in battle; it was the look of a herculean "Front de-Boeuf."

What means the sudden hush—then the scream, as Julia sees the horse stumble, fall, and Bruton Stewart thrown headlong and senseless on the ground. The horse, in attempting to rise, leaped upon the prostrate form.

"Give him air! Don't crowd around him!" cried Latané, the first to reach his side, and a moment later Julia Dearing was also at his side.

They had not a vessel on the seas, not a regiment of veteran troops; no arsenals nor manufactories for making arms and ammunition.

The "Free States," under the slogan of "Union," were battling for the balance of power; the "Slave States," under the slogan of "Liberty," were fighting for independence—repelling invaders—protecting their homes and firesides.

The Constitution of the Confederate States absolutely prohibited the over-sea slave trade; that of the Union did not. The Federals declared that they were fighting to emancipate the negro; the Confederates retorted that the Constitution was the shield of slavery, and that under its protection, they had invested two thousand² of millions of dollars in the "peculiar institution," and that emancipation without compensation meant ruin. The logic of events made slavery the corner-stone of the new government. Meanwhile Washington, Jefferson, and three-fourths of all the Presidents of the United States from the beginning of the government, were slave-holders. Disunion had its origin in New England, now the hot-bed of unionism and abolitionism.

On four separate occasions Massachusetts had threatened to secede from the Union; on one occasion her Legislature had actually passed a vote of secession. One of the chief leaders of the abolitionists on the fourth of July, 1856, undertook to "register a pledge before heaven to do what within him lay to effect the eternal overthrow of the Union." He was now taking an active part in support of the war to maintain that Union.

And yet the father of the Republican party, the great Federalist, Alexander Hamilton, stigmatized coercion of sovereign States as "madness."

American leaders seemed to be political Iconoclasts.

The Union had been the shield of slavery, and the slave-holders now took the initiative in casting aside that shield.

One fought for the rights of the sovereign States; the other for an Imperial Republic.

Thus this clash of arms between these Titans!

Richmond was crowded with troops, officers and office-seekers. Regiments were being marched to their quarters as fast as they arrived from the south. Orderlies galloped through the streets on their errands, and congressmen and ladies mingled with the throng which hurried through the principal thoroughfares. In those early regiments gray-bearded men marched side-by-side with youths and boys hardly in their "teens."

The hardy mountaineer with his trusty rifle laughed at the raillery of the youth at his side, fresh from the mercantile counter, or ridiculed the fancy boots of some parlor-knight who rode, nevertheless, like a veteran cavalryman.

Aides-de-camp, with their glittering uniforms and polished accoutrements, their huge boots reaching nearly to their waists and enclosing their pantaloons, dashing the Texas rowels into the flanks of their steeds, hurried past as if the fate of the country depended on the celerity of their movements. Cavaliers and gay young Southern girls—scions of the "F. F. V.'s"—go dashing past to view the evening dress-parade of the brigade which had so distinguished itself at Manassas. As they pass the General Hospital their gayety is moderated, the speed of their horses is slackened, and hushed voices are eloquent with patriotic meaning.

The heroes of that grand battle are lying there, and the groans of the wounded are heard without the building. In the rear, stretched on tables, lie the desperately wounded to whom chloroform has been administered, and the scalpel of the surgeon is busy amputating limbs and casting them aside with as much *sang-froid* as if these were victims of the *abattoir*, not men and youths from the proudest families of the land.

Side-by-side were ranged the cots throughout the length and breadth of the vast building, and side-by-side lay the factory operative and the heir to a wealthy estate, each a private soldier, each desperately wounded. For, in those gallant days of genuine patriotism, the wealthiest and the

2

most cultured were the first to enlist, and they were singularly free from the desire to rank their fellows, or claim precedence on account of their wealth.

The plowman left his plowshare standing in the field; the mechanic put up his tools for more peaceful times; the professor, the lawyer, the physician, the minister, the student, exchanged the library for the *bivouac* and the battlefield. There were private soldiers, worth hundreds of thousands of dollars, who refused to receive any pay from the government.

Involuntarily, it seemed, the gentlemen of this gay cavalcade took off their hats, and the ladies bowed, as a distinguished looking old gentleman, accompanied by a beautiful young girl, stopped and scanned the portal of a large building as if in doubt as to whether it was the place he was seeking. The girl touched his arm to recall his pre-occupied mind just as the ladies and their escorts, divining the object of his search, had saluted them. With native dignity and stately courtesy he lifted his hat to return the unexpected salutation, but resumed immediately his observations. He was seeking to find a son who had been wounded at Manassas. The wind blew his white hair to and fro as he ascended the steps of the hospital armed with the necessary authority to enter. The surgeon met them at the door, and the face of the kind-hearted physician told them that Hugh's recovery was very doubtful, if not impossible.

" Is he conscious, doctor?" asked Colonel Leslie.

" No, he is under the influence of opiates?"

" Suppose they are discontinued?"

" Delirium would ensue and, perhaps, result fatally. For the present good nursing is our best auxiliary, and we have the best in the world here."

" Let me nurse my poor, darling brother!" said Clara, with an appealing look to the surgeon.

" It would be the worst thing you could do for him, my dear young lady. I appreciate your feelings, but any excitement now will be fatal to your brother."

Clara sank in a chair and sobbed as if her heart would break.

" Can we not see him, doctor?" asked her father.

The surgeon hesitated, then said: " I will not take the

responsibility of refusing, but I caution you, as you value his life, to preserve the utmost quiet; it will not be well if Lieutenant Leslie recognizes you."

Then he slowly preceded them through the hospital. There were hundreds in that building, and the scene, amid the groans of the wounded and the anguish of the dying, attended by the patient care and watchfulness of those white-bonneted Samaritans, the Sisters of Charity, was enough to overcome the stoutest heart. In the quietest corner, near an open window, slept two youths, one dressed in gray, the other in blue.

The first was Hugh Leslie, the second Charles Barnum. the latter dressed in the Federal uniform. Had they not respected Hugh's request that Barnum should be rescued and treated just as he was, the excitement would have killed him. Both were under the influence of morphine. Hugh's face and hands were very pale, his pulse very feeble, himself very quiet. Barnum, in spite of an uglier wound, seemed stronger. Hugh's lips moved, a faint flush came into his cheeks as, half-raising his form, in delirium he uttered a cheer. The gallant boy was fighting the battle over again.

Clara, with irresistible impulse, forgetting her promise, knelt at his side and kissed his pallid brow and lips, and smoothed the hair on that pale, white forehead very carefully that she might not hurt him.

Hugh smiled a sweet, gentle smile and murmured feebly: "Clara, Clara, my gentle sister!" then sank into unconsciousness.

The surgeon lifted her up and drew her away in spite of her violent sobs which seemed about to break her loving heart. Her father, as he neared the door, could only utter: "My poor boy, my poor boy?" The doctor told them that Hugh's life depended on their absenting themselves until the crisis had passed, assuring them that he would warn them in time whatever might be Hugh's fate.

A hen, in gathering her chickens together and sheltering them with her wings, when danger menaces them, cries to them: "Ku-Klux! Ku-Klux!" From so simple a fact originated the name of the dreaded secret society called the Ku-Klux-Klan.

The statutes of the French carbonari were most stringent. The faintest whisper of the secrets of the society to outsiders constituted treason, and was punishable with death. No written communications were permitted. In 1819, there were about 20,000 carbonari in Paris. In 1821, the government was officially informed that the society existed in twenty-five out of the eighty-six departments in France.

The carbonari in Italy and France were republicans. Men like Voyer d'Argenson, Lafayette, Laffitte, Dupont de l'Eure, Barthe, Teste, and other republicans of mark, joined the movement, and adopted the ritual of the Abruzzi carbonari. The *Congrès National* of the Carbonari, which had its headquarters at Paris, seemed for a time omnipotent. All the insurrectionary movements from 1819 to 1822 were attributed to them.

After the July revolution of 1830, the carbonari gave in their allegiance to Louis Philippe. The conservative carbonari do not now exist; but the radical faction founded the new *charbonnerie démocratique*. This carbonari is called *La Commune*. The old *"Commune,"* which acted with the Jacobins and recked with the deeds of Robespierre and Danton, is dead.

The new Commune are "Red Republicans" and Socialists; they are members of the *Societé Internationale*, the members of which are called Nihilists in Russia.

The same discontent, the same violent agitation by revolutionary proletarians, characterized the secret society of Ireland.

The colonel of the 69th New York regiment, and the general commanding the "Irish Brigade" in the Union army, were Fenians. There were 35,000 Fenians regularly enrolled in Ireland in 1858. Catholics in Ireland were prohibited by law from possessing fire-arms. "Circles" were established in all the large American cities, and thousands of soldiers in both the Union and the Confederate armies were Fenians. The Fenian society had its ramifications all over Great Britain and Ireland. A member of the Canadian ministry was killed on the steps of his own door; his opposition to Fenianism was alleged as the motive for the deed. The Duke of Edinburg was dangerously wounded in Port Jackson, Australia.

Carbonari in Italy, the Commune in France, Fenianism in Ireland, Socialism in Germany, Nihilism in Russia, Kukluxism in the Southern States. Well might the question be asked in the United States Senate, "Can you place in penitentiary walls eight millions of people?"

Civil law had been annihilated, and anarchy reigned supreme. Three States now constituted the "Third Military District." Martial law was declared; "Magna Charta" forgotten; the "habeas corpus" Act a nullity.

An ignorant mass of semi-civilized beings, recently emancipated, were being organized in every county in the South into secret societies called "Loyal Leagues." They were taught that their former masters were their oppressors and enemies. The organizers of these "circles," of these "huts," of these "venditas," of these "ventes" in the Southern States were adventurers of the meanest sort; men without principle and without patriotism; men who would have joined the anarchists in Russia, Ireland, Italy or France; men who were not recognized as good citizens or respectable members of society in any part of the United States. The majority of them were penniless adventurers who had not fought in either army. They were called "Scallawags."

When King Louis XVIII. succeeded the exiled Emperor Napoleon in 1817, the people of France were divided into two parties—conquered Imperialists and triumphant Loyalists; but they were Frenchmen, all of the same race, impulses, characteristics and sentiments. Deserters and traitors flaunted the evidence of their paid-for treachery before the disgusted eyes of their compatriots, who had vainly followed the fortunes of their dethroned emperor. Riches followed treachery.

Human nature is the same the world over, and in all times, among all peoples, success is worshipped by the fickle populace eager to cry, "The King is dead; long live the King!"

So it was in the South, and the few white citizens who became suppliant "boot-licks" to the conquerors were enriched with unearned wealth and rewarded for their treachery. They were insolent in their pretensions, arrogant in their professions, mendacious in their reports, and they alone were believed and trusted by the government. Among them Wellington Napoleon Potts was a shining light. But they were a mere handful, while the illiterate, semi-civilized negroes just emerging from slavery were an easy prey to the designing adventurers who assumed all political power. Three typical leaders met. They counselled together. Said one: "Our cause is lost, and I shall leave the country." And the mighty leader, with his shaggy locks and lordly mien, passed away unpardoned and unrepentant to the last. What other country would have allowed him, no longer a citizen of the United States, to hold high office in, and frame the organic laws of, his native State? Another, whose feeble frame held an eagle spirit, dauntless, unselfish, patriotic, humanitarian! the leader in the House of Representatives, as the former was in the Senate of the United States, stood up upon his crutches and calmly said: "I have committed no crime; I shall live quietly at home among my people." Nor could the fetters and disease engendered by prison air break his spirit; and when death came, it found him the Governor of his State and honored throughout the Union.

The third, an ex-State official, as prompt to "bend the knee that thrift might follow fawning," as he was to plunge the people, to whom he was indebted for all that he had, into desperate war, espoused the cause of radicalism and became the richest man in the State. Twelve years before he was an obscure lawyer, poor and almost unknown. Four years before, still poor, he was the universally trusted servant of the people; two years before their heroic civic leader, whose iron will scorned to treat with the enemy on any other basis than the entire independence of the sovereign State, which he seemed to consider, as did Louis XIV., the

kingdom of France, *"L'Etat c'est moi!"* ("The State, it is I!")
And thus was the ballot placed in the hands of ignorant negroes suddenly emancipated.

And yet in many of the Western States the organic law
discriminated directly against the negro, though there was
but one negro to a thousand whites. Even Kansas, which
entered the Union in 1864, during the throes of that bloody
war which was inaugurated on her soil, restricted the right
of suffrage to the white man. Nevada, whose admission to
the Union was subsequent to the enactment of the 13th
amendment, deni d suffrage to "any negro, Chinaman or
mulatto." The question of admitting the negro to suffrage
was submitted to popular vote in Connecticut, Wisconsin
and Minnesota in the autumn of 1865, and at the same time
in Colorado when she was forming her constitution prepara-
tory to seeking admission to the Union, and in all four,
under control of the Republican party at the time, the
proposition was defeated.

In Connecticut only those negroes were allowed to vote
who were admitted freedmen prior to 1818. New York permitted a negro to vote only after he had been a citizen three
years, and for one year the owner of a freehold worth $250,
free of all incumbrances. In the other Northern States
only white men were allowed to vote.

The young negro *valet*, Hallback, was an interesting character in his way. His father's grandfather was said to have been the chief of his tribe before he had been captured and brought to America and sold into slavery. Whether true or false, the effect of this tradition was to give to Hallback a self-esteem not common with his race, and, his pretentions not being received pleasantly by the negroes on the estate, intensified his feeling of isolation.

The fact, too, that education was denied by law to slaves, and that his young master had instructed his sable playfellow in the rudiments of reading and writing, inculcated a morose feeling of discontent in the breast of this young negro slave. But he never complained of his lot, for he could but realize that his very isolation caused a deeper sympathy to be felt and shown him by his mistress and her children than was evinced for the other negroes. He was perfectly black, and, never having labored at hard work, his hands and feet were smaller than those of negroes usually are.

One day after Henry Latané's return home on furlough, he secured a copy of "Uncle Tom's Cabin," and, though it was difficult for him to read it, he did so at night by the lightwood fire in his cabin, and from that day his mind brooded over his situation and condition as a slave. His near relatives were dead, and he had no one in whom he could confide the thoughts which grew like an yeast in his brain until sleep seemed banished from his pillow. There is just enough truth in that wonderful romance to lend conviction to an ignorant mind, eager to believe all that is there related, yet appreciative of the rare kindness which had been his portion all his life.

To his mind every aged butler was another "Uncle Tom," and he felt quite sure that his little mistress, Minnie, was another Eva, blessed with all that lends to human nature its sunniest attributes.

He loved as well as respected Henry Latané, who, whether in camp or in the snow-bounded bivouac, always divided such luxuries as he had with his faithful servant, and ever endeavored to shield him from the post of danger. But Hallback seemed indifferent to danger, and while he took no part in the battles and skirmishes in which his young master was so frequently engaged, he was often under fire, and seemed to court, rather than avoid, danger.

He surprised Henry Latané one day by replying to his order that he should go to the rear: "I will go, Marse Henry, since you order me to; *but I wish I had a country to fight for!*"

Meanwhile he was obedient, submissive and patient, and no one could justly upbraid him for not doing his duty.

After the battles he would request Latané's permission to go out with the ambulance and succor the wounded, and the drivers observed, without objecting, that Hallback seemed particularly solicitous about the wounded Federal soldiers.

In battle animosity gives way before the flash of eternity, which is before every man's eyes, and he is a craven at heart who would not alleviate the sufferings of a gallant foeman after the clash of arms is ended.

  *   *   *   *   *   *   *

He ceased reading, closed the Bible and turned toward Hallback, who had listened attentively and had been evidently impressed.

"Well?" said Hallback.

"Do you not see how powerless we are, and that we are as little birds in the hands of Him?" said Barney, with hand uplifted, while his eyes sought those of his visitor.

"I don't know, Uncle Barney. I don't know anything about the hereafter. It is the ever-living present—the present which sees my race doomed to servitude forever—that oppresses me all the time."

"Then learn to know, my son; to believe is to know. We are powerless. For generations niggers have been slaves in this country. The few free niggers we have among us are no happier than we are. There is Bill Baxter, who owns other niggers, he is not as happy as I am."

"Oh, Uncle Barney, you are not like the rest of us. Everybody respects you, even Mr. Washburn. You don't know what it is."

Taking off his coat, then his shirt, the old man showed

his muscular torso, and there on his bare back were the scars inflicted years before by a brutal overseer's hand. Upon his broad breast were two wounds which seemed to have been inflicted by the knife.

And now the old negro's self posses-ion seemed to fail him, for his breast heaved with terrible excit ment as memory bore him back to the days of his youth, when resistance produced almost fatal wounds. Calming himself, he asked Hallback:

"Are you convinced that I do know what it is?"

"I would never have rested until I had killed the man who did it!" said Hallback.

"Thou shalt not kill. Vengeance is mine, saith the Lord," answered Barney meekly, but fervently.

"Now, Hallback, listen to me. Marst r's brother took my part when I received these wounds, and lost his life in defending me. If he were alive to-day, would it not be my duty to serve him all my life?

"George Washburn killed my nephew in cold blood, and he claims now to be the only friend we poor niggers have. What is my duty toward him?"

"Kill him!" muttered Hallback.

"Hush, my son. Put away such evil thoughts. God, in his own time, will punish him; and you—will you not deserve a like fate if you harbor murder in your heart?"

"But what are we to do?" replied Hallback.

"Wait, and trust in the Lord. He will provide. This war is His doings; and He will treat us as He treated the Israelites."

"What! give us the land?"

"If we deserve it—yes, all that we need. But would you take Marse Henry's land away from him if you could?"

"No; I would not. But I would take Washburn's, and anybody else's land except Marse Henry's."

"Wait, and the land will be given to us."

"But. Uncle Barney, it won't be given to us unless we fight for it, and I have come to tell you good bye: I am going to fight for it."

"Who you gwine to fight, Hall?"

"The Rebels."

"Who is de Rebels?"

" The white folks—the Rebel army—the——"

" Is yer gwine to shoot Marse Henry ?"

Hallback bent his head and the tears forced their way through his fingers, and his sobs prevented an answer.

" It won't do, Hall, my son. For in the absence of your father and mother in heaven, you are my son. I preach to a thousand niggers like you and me, and tell them all what I tell you—we are in the hands of the Lord, and He will provide."

The young negro man stood up now, hat in hand, and said, " Good-bye, Uncle Barney; you don't know, as I do, what will happen soon."

"What gwine to happen, boy ?"

"The Rebels will force all of us young niggers into their army, and we will be shooting at our friends."

A twinkle of humor lighted old Barney's eyes as he asked : "Hall, did you ever see two dogs fight over a bone ?"

"Certainly I have; why do you ask me that question ?"

" Well, then, did you ever see the bone fight ?"

A broad smile, followed by laughter, was Hallback's answer as he saw the force of the old preacher's parable, and he took his depature in a better frame of mind than he had had for a long time.

The old Federal road ran along the west side of the premises at "Chestnut Hill," and near it was the garden, and the house of the gardener, old Zeke. Like most of his race, Zeke talked to himself while alone at work, or sang lowly portions of hymns peculiar to African hymnology.

He frequently talked to the fowls, which crowded around him, eager to get anything which he might bestow upon them.

On the day selected by Barnum for his adventure, the old man had admitted some pet hens into the garden, "to help me rake it, chickens," he affirmed. He would dig a few spades full of earth, carefully turning it over each time, the poultry watching him as if deeply interested in his investigations.

"Whar all de wurms gone to, chickens?" he asked. Then he dug again, and threw toward them the worms.

"You'se all de same age—you is—and you kin jist fight over dem wurms; fust come, fust sarved is de rule." After a while a cock, which had been trying to get into the garden, succeeded in flying over the fence and dispersing the hens, as he rapidly executed that political maxim, "to the victor belong the spoils," pursuing finally a hen that had not succeeded in swallowing her prize. Old Zeke raised his head, keeping his foot on the spade meanwhile, and looking around said: "What dat racket 'bout?" Then he spied the cock. "Whar did you cum frum, rooster? Git out o' here you blasted nigger, you!" and then the old man chased the contumacious rooster; now throwing clods of earth, now a hoe, then a stone, always missing the object of his wrath, until his breath was exhausted. "I'll fix you yit, you triflin' varmint!" said the old negro, shaking his head and fist at the cock, which had taken refuge in the raspberry bushes first, and then had made its exit. There were the strawberry beds and asparagus beds, mashed down by the old fellow in his angry chase, and there the grape-vines torn down, fully a week's labor, caused by the irruption of this piratical rooster. As the old man surveyed the scene of confusion in this sacred precinct, which he ruled like a despot, quarreling even with his master if he ordered any changes to be made or new plants introduced without first consulting him, he got more and more indignant.

The chickens crowded around him again, and old Zeke thus endeavored to console them : "Never mind, chickens, dat rooster 'll never bodder you no more; I 'clare 'fore God he wont!" The chickens seemed delighted. Then going to the fence, he leaned on it, and cried : "Hezekiah! Oh, Hez! Oh, Hez! you Hezekiah! Come here, nigger!" Then he muttered to himself: "Drat dat chile; 'pears 's if he ain't got no more p'liteness dan-dan a rooster."

"Hello!" said a voice on the other side of the fence. As old Zeke looked around he saw the tall form of a travel-stained man, evidently a "tramp," dressed in a dilapidated suit of jeans. The man held a carpet-bag in his hand and a roll of blanket under one arm.

"Hello!" repeated the stranger.

"Hello, yourself!" ejaculated old Zeke.

"I'm tollerable; how's your family?"

"Four wives buried, and a huntin' of a young gal now what wants ter marry—sixteen chillun, ten of 'em gals, or women ruther, and fifty-two grand-chillun; all well, thank ye. How mout be yourn, stranger?"

The stranger laughed. "You seem pretty well satisfied, old man," said he.

"Seemin's lying, den; dat's what 'tis," said Zeke.

"Then you are not satisfied?" queried the man.

"In course I ain't. Ain't I wukked to death? And den dese here tarnal roosters and chillun what won't heer nothin' and won't mind nothin' what dey *do* heer's nuff to drive me 'stracted! Sartinly, I ain't satisfied. Ain't I done raised two craps o' chillun fur marster? and here I is, wukkin yit!"

"That does seem pretty hard. Who lives here, old man?"

"Why, marster lives here," replied old Zeke, "and me and a heap o' niggers.

"Who is your marster, my friend?" (Particular stress laid on the last two words.)

"Look a here, stranger, whar *did* you come from, anyhow? Is you from K'liny?" (Carolina). Evidently old Zeke considered it a phenomenon for a man not to know who Col. Leslie was. Before the man could reply old Zeke caught sight of a boy. Now a boy is generally suggestive of broken china or other evidences of destructive powers, and the boy whom old Zeke saw was not an exception. "You Hez, come here to me, sir, you good for nothin' brat!" The boy came on, making faces at the stranger meanwhile, and Zeke resumed his conversation with that individual. Said he: "Folks ain't what dey use to was, no how. Dat dere boy's 'nuff to drive me 'stracted."

"What has he been doing?" asked the man.

Old Zeke paused and scratched his head to answer this unexpected question. The boy had arrived, however, and relieved his embarrassment. Said he: "Hez, why didn't you come when I fust called you? Why don't you mind me, boy?"

"I didn't hear you," replied the boy, grinning with mischief, as he caught the stranger's eye.

"Why didn't you hear me? What's yer eers made fur?" asked the old patriarch.

"I was hidin' de pig," said the boy, showing his ivories. As the boy said this he dodged, and as he dodged the old man threw a "chunk o' wood," as he called it, at the urchin. "I'll chunk yer life out'en you, boy! G'long wid you, nigger, and ketch dat rooster. Ef I ketch him in here agin, I'm gwine to take de hide off e'n you!" Hezekiah grinned, cracked his heels together, turned a somersault, and ran back to the cabin. He had betrayed a weakness of the old man's, viz., stealing a fat pig occasionally. In old Zeke's case such thefts were intentionally not discovered.

"'Pears to be a smart boy," said the stranger.

"Yes, he's right peart, Hez. is; but de wust chile in de world!" said the old man, looking fondly at his favorite grand-child, who was clapping his hands to his legs, imitating the sound of a horse running, as he ran back to the cabin.

"You say your marster is unjust to you—why don't you get your marster to sell you?"

"I've axed him to many en' many a time; he won't do it; he can't spare old Zeke. Marster wouldn't take two thousand dollars fur me."

"Are you more valuable than the other old men?"

"Sartainly I is; makin' truck (i. e. gardening) is one thing, and plowin' an' hoein's another. Who gwine to wukk dis ere gyardin if Zeke ain't here? Now tell me dat."

"Don't the other old men work as hard as you do?"

"Stranger, whar did you come frum? Sartainly not. I works harder'n any on 'em. Dere's Pompey; he's two years older'n me. He don't do nothin' but shoot crows for marster, an' ducks and squirrels fur hisself. Dere's Club-foot Harry; he makes baskits in de fall fur to pick cotton in, an' he suns hisself de balance of de year. Dere's Cary; he don't do nothin' but make horse-collars and drive de horse kyart (cart). Dere's Gumbo; he feeds de mules an' tends stock. And dere's Big Dick, an' ole Mose, an' Yaller Bill, an' Step, an' Jake, an' Long Tom, an' a heap more on 'em what don't do nothin' 't all, year in and year out."

"Who feeds and clothes them?"

"Marster. I say, mister, got a chaw terbacker?"

The stranger, like all poor people, did manage to save enough to provide this luxury, and he gave old Zeke a quid, or, in his parlance, a "chaw."

"And yet he forces you to work?" suggested the tramp.

"Look-a-here, mister, to tell you de God's trufe, marster don't do no sich thing. He jest says, says he, 'Zeke;' says I, 'Sir!' Says he, 'Zeke, you go down to Oswichee and live there, and I'll try to get some one else to take your place here; but I know I will never be able to find anybody what knows as much about gyardenin' as you does.'" Says I, 'Marster, you an' me is a most wore out, we is; an' dis ere gyarden done b'long to me so long I hates to leave it.'"

"If he would give you your freedom, my friend, would you leave it?"

Old Zeke slowly approached the man, looked at him closely and said: "Look a here, mister, who is you, anyhow? I done found out already dat you ain't none o' our kind o' folks. Whar did you come frum?"

The man put his fingers to his lips in token of silence, bowed, and pointed to Zeke's cabin.

"All right!" said Zeke in a confidential tone, "you go to de cabin."

Then he sang in a loud voice a revival hymn, working industriously meanwhile, until finally he gathered up his tools, put them on his shoulder, assumed an expression of extra innocence, and continued his song until he reached the cabin.

Arrived at the cabin, after putting his tools in a corner, the old negro went to the door and looked out cautiously to see if any one was visible; then re-entered the cabin, and with a chuckle of satisfaction, slapped the tramp familiarly on the back, and extended his right hand. "Glad to see you sir, I is. What's de news frum Mr. Washburn?" Before the stranger could reply old Zeke had deposited himself in a chair which Hezekiah had placed there for him, and almost immediately he jumped up again, with the angry expression: "What! whar dat chile?" rubbing himself meanwhile as if in pain. "He's de aggravatenist chile onhung!"

The mystery was soon explained. The boy had placed a red hot piece of iron in the chair just as the old man sat down; and as soon as he saw how the charm worked, had taken himself off, with the peculiar delight which boys feel in having done a mischievous thing.

The tramp could not conceal his amusement. But a matter of too great importance was before old Zeke now to pay any more attention to Hezekiah.

"Well, old man, I think you'll have to get your master to sell that boy," said the stranger.

"Dar 'tis agin! Marster won't sell no nigger onless he wants to be sold, and Hez. don't. He wants to stay here to pester me." The truth was the old man had begged his "marster" to let him have the boy to "wait on him," as he expressed it: and he would have sooner parted with his hand than with Hezekiah, who made life spicy for him.

"You do seem to have your troubles. What's your name?"

"Zeke."

"Mr. Zeke," continued the man, "don't you want to be free?"

"'Deed I does," said Zeke, and inspired by that suggestive prefix, "mister," the old man continued: "I tell you what, I wish I was free!"

"That's my business in these parts, Mr. Zeke. I wish to set you all free," replied the stranger.

"Hi! how you gwine ter do it?"

"Will you help me, Mr. Zeke?"

"Will I help *you* to help *me?* Sartainly I will."

"Well, you tell all the old men like yourself to meet me at Ringgold with their children and their children's children, and I will lead them to Ohio, and you'll all be free; that's what this war is for."

"Golly!" said Zeke, smiling at the prospect. "Will dey give us all houses to live in, an' carriages an' hosses, an' niggers—no, we don't want no niggers. What do dey do fur niggers up dar?"

"No, we will not give you houses, nor horses, nor servants, but we will give you freedom, my friend."

"What good freedom gwine to do us widout de means of 'joyin' it?" queried Zeke.

"You must work and make a living," said the man.

"Hi! ain't dat what we does here? 'ceptin' 'tis de ole men and women an' de blind an' 'flicted folks—dey don't do no wukk here. Will dey have to wukk dar?"

"Yes, my friend, all able-bodied men must work there. We will try to provide for each head of a family forty acres and a mule, for which he can pay when he makes money enough."

"Look-a-here, Mister, what's yer name? we don't want no mule to work wid. I want a bob-tail white hoss, like marster's, an' I don't want to do nuthin' but ride him 'bout, and give orders to niggers, like marster does.

"Marster's free, he don't wukk. Bill Baxter is a free nigger and he owns his own land and he aint no better off 'an we is, 'ceptin' 'tis he goes and comes whar and when he pleases."

"Would'nt you like to be able to do that too, Mr. Zeke?"

"Sartainly, I would; *pervidin, mind you,* Marster would let me come home when I got tired cavortin' 'round, and would take keer of me when I git so I can't take keer uv myself."

3

"Then you won't take any risk to secure your freedom?"

"Sartainly I wont! I don't want no freedom whar I got to wukk at my time uv life," said Zeke

"But the young men will be glad to make the effort, will they not?" asked the tramp.

"I 'speck dey will; de very last one on em! All young folks is fools, white and black, 'ceptin tis Miss Clara, bless de honey's soul!"

"Who is Miss Clara?" said the man with increasing interest and a change in his tone.

"What yer want ter know dat fur? She is too high quality fur *you* ter know, but she'd meet you like she meets evrybody, white an' black, so kind-like dat dey all loves de chile; whv, Miss Clara's my young Missus," said Zeke.

"Is she pretty?"

"De angels in heben can't beat her!" exclaimed the old man.

"What do you think about this war, Mr. Zeke?"

"I think dey kilt mars Hugh, an' mighty nigh kilt dat tother young man who dey do say —leastawise Mariar do say it—is a Yankee soldier hisself! but I don't b'lieve it."

"Why don't you believe it?" said the tramp.

"'Cause he acts like de quality-folks, like a gentleman—an I don't b'lieve no white-folks kin be quality onless dey owns niggers"

"Does he own negroes?"

"Dat's why Mariar say he is a Yankee. But I will tell you what, Mister-what's-yer-name," said Zeke growing confidential again, as if he was about to impart some very important information, "he's gwine to own lots on 'em some day."

"What do you mean?" said the stranger, leaning forward.

"I mean he's a courtin' of Miss Clara, dat's what I mean; and she has nussed him, and rid wid him nigh on to two months. Now, mister, hit stands to reasin dat when a gal does dat, she's gwine to fall in love afore she knows it. Lord sakes alive! won't Mars Harry be mad den?" said old Zeke, laughing to himself.

"Who on earth is this "Mars Harry?" said the man.

"Mars Harry Latané, what owns, or is gwine to own, de place jinin' ourn down to Etowah, on de river. He's a quality-gentleman fur you! an ef he knowed what was gwine on here, he'd leff his company, an de war, and he'd take dat ar Mr. Barnum an lift him out'en his boots afore he could say Jack Robinson!" and the old man laughed immoderately at the imaginary picture.

The tramp's hat had fallen off now, also his wig, and his features were disguised only by the whiskers, though he did not seem to know it. "I clar to gracious!" cried old Zeke, looking intently at the man. "Great snakes alive! ef you aint him!" And then old Zeke informed him that he intended to tell his master on him, "Onless," he added confidentially, "you kin prove to me Mr. Washburn sent you here."

Barnum's intense interest had betrayed him, but, assuming a careless manner and re-adjusting his wig and whiskers, he took up his bundle and departed, first telling old Zeke that he would notify Mr. Washburn, if he reported him, and asserting that he did not intend to be picked up for another man. Old Zeke remained in deep thought for a few moments. He was not positive about this being Barnum, and in spite of all his statements there was not a negro on the estate, old or young, who would not gladly have accepted freedom. Then he concluded he would tell his "marster" any way that Barnum would not do as a suitor for Clara's hand.

Col. Leslie intercepted old Zeke as he was on his way to the house, and began to make complaints against Hezekiah. "I tell you what, Zeke," said he, "I've spared that little darkey long enough, and the next time he strikes my pointer, I intend to thrash him. I don't believe you ever do whip him." "Marster, in course you kin whip Hez—in course you kin whip *me*, whenever you wants to, in course you kin! But did you *see* Hez strike de dog?"

"No, Zeke, if I had, I should have whipped him anyhow, but somebody has struck Dan."

"Dar 'tis!" said Zeke, "dar 'tis! now marster, you is de court, and you is de jedge, and you is de jury: which one am you, when you make up your mind to whip Hez, jest because Mariar's chile has hit de pineter?"

"Zeke, I do beleive you have got a way of looking right into me. I had made up my mind to whip Hez this time, and have come here for that purpose, but you have put a question to me, which I can't answer. Now, did you see Maria's boy hit my dog?"

"I seed him hit your dog jest as much as you seed Hez hit de pineter," replied the old man. "I tell you what, marster, jest bekase Hez is a peart, lively critter, dese niggers charges all dere rascalities up to him, but bless your heart, marster, dat Hez's de innocentest boy I ever seed!"

Detaining the old man long enough to admit of Barnum's return to the house, Col. Leslie slowly entered it, but was called back by Zeke.

Barnum had returned and had taken off the old clothing which he had worn over his best suit, and was now describing his interview to the young ladies in the parlor, omitting, however any reference to Clara, or the cause of Zeke's suspicion.

Then they heard old Zeke's voice addressing Col. Leslie, who was sitting in the veranda.

"I say, marster," said Zeke.

"What now, Zeke?"

"Marster, you has been imposed on," solemnly said old Fidelity.

"By whom, Zeke?"

"By a man you can't put no 'pendence on—a piece of white-trash, sir."

"What do you mean, Zeke? who has given you a dram?"

"I aint had no dram, marster, sence de war commenced; you's got so stingy you ought to be shamed o' yourself! I done forgot de very taste uv whisky. But, marster, spite o' your stinginess, I'll tell you how you's been posed on. You has done like de man what de Bible tells 'bout: one cold, frosty mornin' he found a snake in de big road, what was froze stiff. He tuk de snake home wid him, an warmed hit by de fire, an hit bit him an pizened him!" said the old negro with the solemnity of a judge.

"Well, nobody has poisoned me," said his master.

"Dey has tried to, sir, but old Zeke—"

"Who has tried to poison me?" interrupted Col. Leslie, not wishing to hear Zeke's history of his faithful services which he had heard already a hundred times.

"Dat dere young man wat come here wid you atter mars

Hugh died, and what Miss Clara an you has warmed to life agin!" said the old darkey.

"Who? Barnum! Why, Zeke, you *are* drunk. Barnum was Hugh's best friend."

"He ain't no friend o' yourn, marster; an he aint quality, marster; an he aint fitten to cut mars Harry Latané out, marster!"

Then old Zeke related all that had transpired, but Barnum had his reasons for wishing to put a stop to his narrative before the old negro reached that part of the recital which related to his interest in Clara. He therefore walked out on the veranda from the parlor window and talked laughingly to Clara Leslie and her friends, as if he had not heard a word he had said

"I 'clar to God!" said Zeke, staring with wonder at the unexpected appearance of the young gentleman dressed in his elegant suit of black, his easy manners, and the laughing eye which accompanied the following request, addressed to old Zeke:

"Proceed with your story, uncle Zeke, it is interesting to hear one's self denounced. But, really, I can't understand why you should dislike me so much as to invent that story."

He only said: "I 'clar to God, marster! fore God, I don't b'lieve 'twas him no how!" and retired completely mystified. He walked slowly back to his cabin in deep thought, then went to the road and endeavored to track the tramp, but he finally gave it up, completely "out done," as he expressed it. His boasts had already subjected him to ridicule so often that he concluded to keep his own counsel henceforth concerning the mysterious stranger. But he humbly begged Barnum's pardon the next time he saw him for having mistaken him for a tramp.

Barnum informed him that his fidelity to his master had raised him very much in his estimation.

(NOTES FROM A JOURNAL.)

Death lurked behind every hillock, nay every bush, green and fair to look upon the summer day when peace charms the landscape, but treacherous and sinister as the eye of a serpent when war plants a weapon there!

From the summit of Kennesaw I viewed the glowing landscape as the foot-hills of the Blue Ridge recede away in the distance; I saw puffs of white smoke, a sign I knew full well, and then the loud report of the Parrot guns planted on yonder hill a quarter of a mile away.

Opposite us is the summit of Pine Mountain, and three Generals commanding our troops survey the scene from the outpost there. They are joined later by a Cavalry Brigadier transferred like myself from Virginia for the campaign in his native State. But one of those Generals can compare in splendid physique with Bruton Stewart, and that is the loved Bishop of Louisiana, Lieutenant General Leonidas Polk. The smallest in stature is the master-mind and great commander who, though pressed back gradually, inflicted a loss of ten to one upon the enemy, and in whom the confidence of all his troops was unbounded. A signal flag is waved from yonder height, and our signal sergeant answers the signal.

"What! General Polk killed! and by that battery a quarter of a mile away!" The sergeant is up again, field glasses are again directed toward the outpost; the flag flashes in the sun light with rapidity as the signals are exchanged, like the talking between two deaf mutes.

"Yes, a cannon ball passed through General Polk's chest, from left to right, killing him instantly," said Col. Harris, Inspector-General of the army, to me. We bore him down the mountain side, and in the rear of a store in the village he was laid, the most perfect picture of manly serenity and physical beauty I ever saw in a man of his age.

"Two hours ago," said Bruton Stewart to me, "he gave me instructions, and I was to report to him by daylight to-morrow. Truly—" Then he ceased, for why should two old soldiers, though young men who had "faced the music" a score of times and more, why should we moralize about the uncertainty of life?

Two hours later we were at the front again, and a blaze of fire ran up and down the sides and heights of Kennesaw, now direct, now "*en zig-zag*," now to the right, then to the left, until that human tide is repelled and cast down the mountain sides. And a thousand died there.

Both armies in line of battle, and the long, seemingly continuous stretch of canvas in the distance, is the Federal wagon train. Away to the right is a cavalry skirmish; to the left the opposing batteries are hotly engaged. And yonder, trending away toward the blue horizon the ranges of mountains, grow fainter and fainter as coming twilight shuts out a scene where nature has painted her fairest landscapes, and the demon of war has let loose the lurid flames that are grander than any pyrotechnic display; more terrible than any scene peace can offer; but exciting to the true soldier as is the spirit of speed to the race-horse about to enter the arena.

There "Old Rock" illustrated this spirit of battle when his horse was killed from under him; and, leaping off, he is seen cutting the harness away from a horse attached to a caisson, and then mounting him bareback, with hoarse, rough voice, he rallies and leads on his men—men, than whom never braver fought in defense of their native land!

I see again, from the roof of the old Military Institute building, itself on the highest hill, the lights and the red flag of the signal station on the heights of Kennesaw. The low distant rumbling of artillery comes sounding through the night air. Our boys are doing their duty there!

Again I wander in the park in the village, where beaux and belles used to congregate and laugh the merry hours away. It is filled now with cots upon which recline the maimed heroes who have fallen during the battles now raging around Marietta,

But a few days ago General Hart led our brigade with sabre waving over his head, and gallant cheers answered his beckoning challenge until we halted after a glorious victory!

Across this very park we dashed.

Ah! but the counter-picture! my young friend William Young, but eighteen years old, and the picture of manly beauty before that charge. With the gay bravery of a Southern soldier, uninfluenced by thought of office or promotion, this wealthy young gentleman gloriously illustrated the private soldier.

I asked: "Who did you say was mortally wounded, Colonel?" And a great grief welled up in my heart as Thompson answered, "William Young."

There he lies, mortally wounded, but unconquered still, and murmuring, as I raise his head and give him a drink of water from my canteen : "It is the fate of war!"

Near him is a Federal soldier, also mortally wounded, and he, too, receives the attention which "soldier metes to soldier;" and although the noblest and bravest private in our brigade is wounded unto death, no word of unkindness is spoken near that fallen foeman.

Again the shrill whistle of rifle and minnie balls come over railway embankment, and the fight is joined in full view of Institute Hill.

A moment later, and Thompson is himself borne to the rear, shot in the head.

But in battle all thoughts are merged in the one triumphant thought of victory; and a yell, followed by a dashing charge, greets again our brigade commander as he rises in his stirrups and smiles when he sees the effect of our shells and canister.

And a few days later the Commanding General reported, in alluding to Bruton Stewart's fierce, stubborn fight a few miles distant, "The right of the Federal army made a change of front by which it faced to the east. It was opposed in this maneuvre by Stewart's cavalry, as well as 2,500 men can resist 30.000." * * * *

I was standing in the dépôt at Atlanta. The bomb shells from the Federal army could be seen bursting as they penetrated the walls of the great buildings near it. But pshaw! this was a daily occurrence, and we were quite accustomed to it. But what moved me more than anything else, was the sight of hundreds of soldiers who leaned on their mus-

kets and wept! It is true; some cursed; others looked un-
uttered curses; many, many others wept.

Why? The great General whom all trust has been removed from the command of the army. That was all.

Thirty-six thousand Confederates, of whom six thousand
were without arms, was the effective force of the Confederate army at Dalton in 1864. The odds were ten to four
against them. This force was increased until it numbered
37,652 infantry, 2.812 artillery, with 112 guns, and 2,392
cavalry.

Opposed to them was an army of 98,797 men and 254
guns. To this force was added three divisions of cavalry,
numbering 11.000 men. In the rear of the Federals were
119,000 enlisted men, fit for duty, which could be drawn
upon freely if reinforcements should be needed.

Why speak of "the continuous battle from June 10th to
July 2nd?"

Why speak of the incessant artillery fire for twenty-six
days around Kennesaw mountain?

Why speak of the exploit, greater than any which the
ancient Fabius ever executed, of conducting this army of 43,-
000 men one hundred miles, fighting almost daily forces
nearly three times as numerous and infinitely better
equipped, without the loss of a single wagon?

Over 10,000 Federal dead are buried near the base of that
mountain, silent witnesses to heroic valor.

General Johnston has been removed. That is but the
loss of the services of one commander. But it was infinitely more depressing than all the toiling marches; the lack
of shoes and comforts; the lack of ammunition and arms;
the series of daily battles and continuous retreat.

The one thing the army *did not lack* was confidence in the
wisdom and ultimate success of their general.

"Of what avail the long siege," men asked one another
"If *he* is removed, who can lead us to victory?"

But they did not murmur, and they fought as men only
fight who battle in defense of their homes.

It was the energy of heroism incarnated.

*   *   *   *   *   *   *   *

And this "Gate City" stands on "holy ground." Within
it during that siege rare scenes were daily enacted.

Here and there a straggling Confederate might be seen silently viewing the wanton destruction with feelings "too deep for utterance." Now a cavalryman, with his blanket, carbine, and high-topped cavalry boots, would turn and watch the bursting shells as a "hole" is made in the wall of some prominent building, and then, sticking spurs to his horses flanks, give a "rebel yell" and dash on to the front.

Upon the outer streets no vehicles are to be seen save those unmistakable signs of war: ambulances, with the sick, wounded, or dead, and gun-carriages, whose sombre mien is enlivened by the laughing voices of light-hearted artillery-men.

They were dressed in dingy jeans, but, for all that, were as invincible as if clad in armor. Grand old uniform! what if it was dingy and rough, "A man's a man for a' that," and *these be men indeed!*

There are the long lines of infantry in the entrenchments that envelope the gate city which *can not be taken.*

We feel it in our bones; indeed we *know* that this town can-not be taken by assault by a force ten times as numerous as ours. They stretch all around Atlanta with similar interior lines, and, amid the constant firing, the men joke and laugh with the utmost *bonhomie.*

The 22nd of July! I will not recall that gallant Confede-rate victory save to describe two scenes that will be indelibly impressed upon the retina until life shall end. One, as the moving army is making the circuit around Decatur: I see that wonderful and indefatigable leader, Pat. Cleburne. He rises in his stirrups and orders the column to " close up!" as we neared the scene of battle. No one who saw him can for-get his splendid appearance that day, rough but glorious child of war! As Cleburne's division entered the field, their General close behind the centre, the ranks parted and the heroic leader now rode in front of the centre and cried: " For-ward! charge! follow me!" And resistless as an avalanche was the onset, as he repelled the enemy and drove them from the entrenchments, though they were ten lines deep. They were struck by the flower of the Army of Tennessee, led by Cleburne, just as General Walker, the chivalric son of Georgia, with flashing eyes and splendid mien, leads his column by our corps, and we give him a yell which reverberates above the battle roar.

A few hours later General Walker was killed, but he will ever live in the minds of those who saw him that fatal day.

The other scene was enacted by a mere boy, a youthful *aide-de-camp* to our general of division. We had captured the batteries opposed to our immediate command and a large number of prisoners, when, in the very midst of our triumph, we were ordered to fall back. Why we were so ordered we never could learn. The enemy, seeing this, and realizing the great disparity in force, advanced on three sides at once. Before we knew it we were nearly surrounded, and demoralization was apparent in our ranks. It seemed that our whole brigade would be captured, and the Texans to our left also. The color-bearer of the division, borne back by the common impulse as the lines swayed back and forth, sought safety behind a large oak tree. It was then that this young *aide-de-camp* dashed up with the news that reinforcements were at hand.

But the color-bearer of that magnificent division, for the first time in his life perhaps, seemed dazed, bewildered, unable to grasp the meaning of the order of this boy to go forward. Bomb-shells were bursting overhead, or ploughing the ground, or scattering the missiles of death in the air. Minnie balls were thick as hail, it seemed, and countless forms, the gray and the blue, lying close together, dotted the road and field.

"Go forward with that flag!" shouted the dauntless youth.

"I can't. See! our line is far to the rear," replied the color-bearer.

"Forward! I say. Reinforcements are at hand. We must rally these troops!"

The soldier hesitated.

I held my breath as I saw the *aide-de-camp* pull his pistol from the holsters, cock it, and present it to the soldier's head. There were hundreds lying there, dead or dying or grievously wounded, but they were shot in battle by the enemy, and one does not stop to think of the man who has fallen just as his elbow touches one's own, so wonderful is the hold of the battle-spirit in the midst of the carnage. And all these fallen men moved me not. But this scene, when a mere youth—

his eyes and every feature the very incarnation of battle—was about to send a bullet crashing through the brain of a brave Confederate soldier—for none but the brave are made division color-bearers—paralyzed me for the moment.

I held my breath and waited.

Then came the voice of the color-bearer: "If you are so damned brave, take the flag and rally them yourself!"

I felt that no other appeal could have saved his life, but that one did.

With a smile of disdain he replaced his pistol, and amid that hail of cannister, calmly said: "I will do it, give it to me!"

And gloriously did he do it! He did not look back to see whether one man followed him, but he moved forward, holding that grand old tattered standard erect amid the storm. Too young or too feeble, for he already seemed physically exhausted, to hold it with one arm, he dropped the reins, and guiding his mare by his knees and feet, held the flag forward with both hands and gallantly moved direct upon the enemy's works.

Horse and rider seemed animated by a common impulse, and that was to *get there!* And now a yell that was begun on the right of the line reached the centre, and, like wave on wave of sound, passed along the line to the farthest man on the left, as they turned as if on dress-parade and rushed forward to rally around that standard!

The tremendous odds against them were forgotten as they saw that dauntless boy move steadily forward. They faced the front and fought with desperate valor, as the entrenchments were taken and lost again and again. To the right and to the left they turned, and stood at bay, and repelled the enemy. And just as the field is won, the horse and rider, still holding the division standard and still in advance of all, go down, as a grape-shot tears its way through the flank of the noble animal which has borne him so well. But the flag does not touch the ground, for, amid all that dreadful carnage the color-bearer has walked behind that horse, eager to regain what he had given up, and fearless of danger, That flag had seemed to him country, home, wife, children—but another now bore it, and the veteran of fifty battles followed it aimlessly. As the gallant youth fell, still holding it with both hands, the color-bearer reached for it, and said: "Give it to me now. I can carry it!" Leaping from the dust, and wiping away that which obscured his vision, the *aide-de-camp* looked to see who this could be who would rob him of this proud privilege. As he saw and recognized the color-bearer, and remembered how nearly he had acted as his executioner, he said: "I yield it to you, but to no one else will I surrender it." And gallantly did that soldier retrieve himself.

And now the young hero was a boy again, for tears came into his eyes as he saw before him the expiring agonies of the noble steed which had borne him all through the Kentucky campaign, and thence through Tennessee and Georgia. If ever eyes bade mortal farewell forever. the eyes of that faithful animal spoke its speechless grief at parting from its young master.

Can yonder round-shouldered, stooping convict be Hall-back? Poor fellow! Drawn irresistibly to his vicinity, without intending it I came in the line of his vision. How instantaneous the change! Like a lightning flash the gloomy, sullen look of despair gáve way to the old light, as his eyes flashed the intelligence that he had but two years more to serve. And then? Ah! there is now no kind, wise, humane old Barney to place his hand upon his shoulder and bid him ".wait." Wait! "For eighteen years, Marse Henry!" and then the great tears rolled down his deeply-lined face, and agony was depicted there such as I never wish to see again. Then, dashing them aside, and wringing my hand affectionately, the dogged, sullen, despairing look resumed control of his features, and the pick went up and down, up and down, with regular, horrible monotony, as up and down it had gone on thus for eighteen years.

How changed is he, the once bright and earnest young man, filled with the laudable ambition to lead his dependent race to a higher civilization.

NOTE.

Applications for agencies for the sale of this book should be made to the Secretary of the Fulton County Veterans' Association, box 163, Atlanta, Ga. As Confederate Veterans will be the chief beneficiaries, they are invited to solicit subscriptions, for which they will receive commissions on each book sold. The book will contain 300 pages.

9 7 8 3 3 3 7 3 4 6 8 7 4